YOU CAN NEVER RUN OUT OF LOVE

Helen Docherty and Ali Pye

SIMON & SCHUSTER

London   New York   Sydney   Toronto   New Delhi

You can run out of biscuits . . .

Or run out of bread.

You can run out of energy,

flopped on your bed.

You can run out of chocolates

(none left in this box).

When the washing piles up,

you can run out
of socks.

You can run out of time.

You can run out
of money.

You can run out of patience,

when things don't seem funny. BUT . . .

You can never (no never, not ever),

you can **never**
run out of **LOVE**.

You can run out of milk.

You can run out of jelly.

If you run out of nappies,

things can get smelly!

You can run out of glue.

You can run out of soap.

When you know it's too late,

THE END

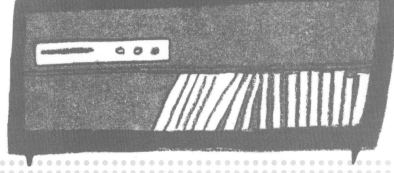

you can run out of hope.

On a very bad day, you can run out of luck . . .

Or run out of ideas,

and get really stuck. BUT . . .

You can never (no never, not ever),

you can never
run out of LOVE.

Love doesn't come
in a bottle or jar.

It's right there inside you,
wherever you are.

You don't have to charge it.
No batteries inside.

Your love can be BIG,
as the whole world is wide.

You can't measure love in a bucket or cup.

You don't have to worry you'll use it all up.

'Cos love's not a game, where you have to keep score.

Whenever you give some,

you'll always have more.

When you've run out of everything else,

you'll still find . . .

you can **never** run out of LOVE.

Space Pirates

and the Treasure of Salmagundy

Scoular Anderson

FRANCES LINCOLN CHILDREN'S BOOKS

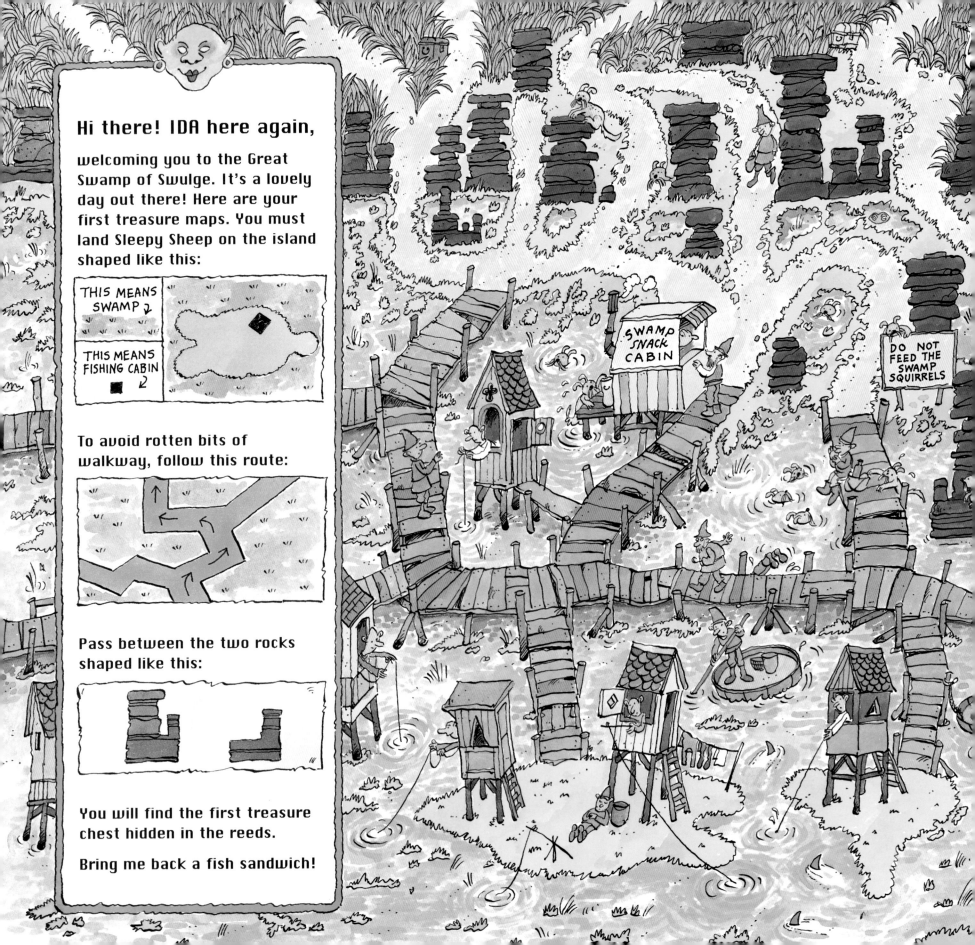

Hi there! IDA here again,

welcoming you to the Great Swamp of Swulge. It's a lovely day out there! Here are your first treasure maps. You must land Sleepy Sheep on the island shaped like this:

THIS MEANS SWAMP ↓

THIS MEANS FISHING CABIN ↓

To avoid rotten bits of walkway, follow this route:

Pass between the two rocks shaped like this:

You will find the first treasure chest hidden in the reeds.

Bring me back a fish sandwich!

SWAMP SNACK CABIN

DO NOT FEED THE SWAMP SQUIRRELS

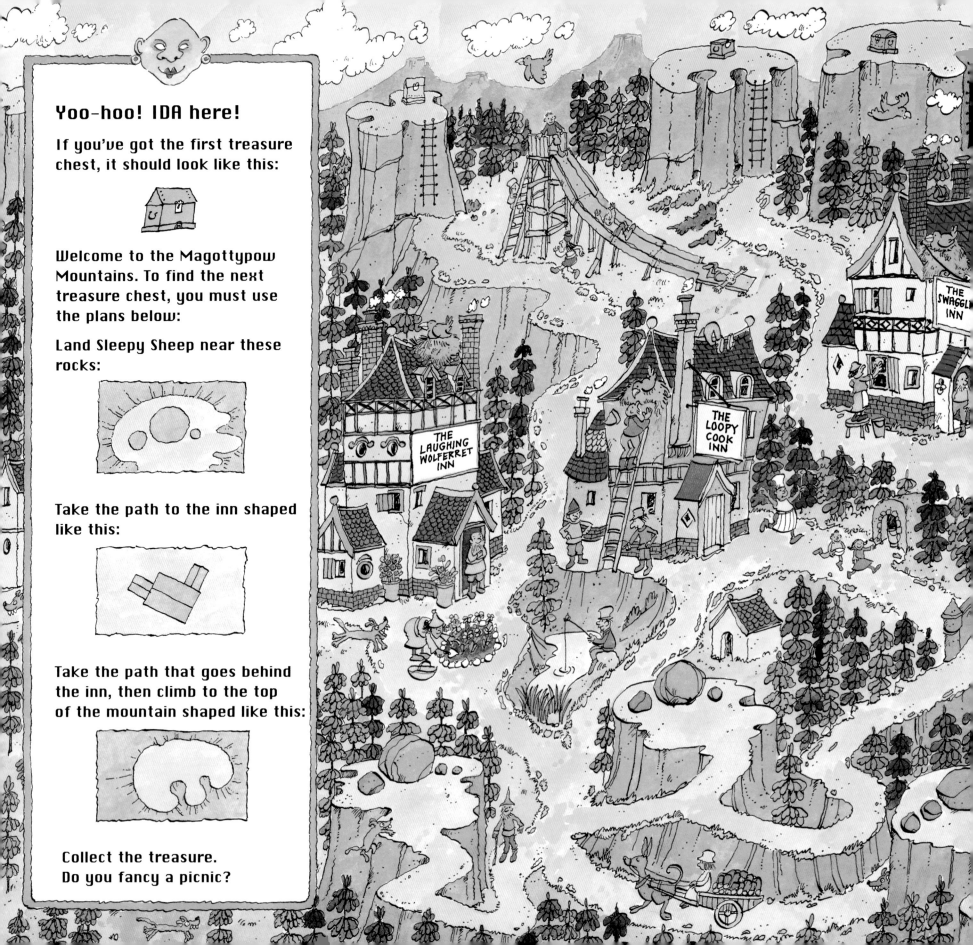

Yoo-hoo! IDA here!

If you've got the first treasure chest, it should look like this:

Welcome to the Magottypow Mountains. To find the next treasure chest, you must use the plans below:

Land Sleepy Sheep near these rocks:

Take the path to the inn shaped like this:

Take the path that goes behind the inn, then climb to the top of the mountain shaped like this:

Collect the treasure.
Do you fancy a picnic?

Hi-ya! IDA speaking.

If you got the right treasure chest from the mountain, it should look like this:

You are now at the Wittery Waterfalls. Here's what you have to do:

Land Sleepy Sheep on the back of this fall hog (it's OK, they sleep for months).

Climb to the top of the right-hand steps. Take the left-hand path as far as the plumberry-picker's hut.

Cross the bridge that goes behind the waterfall.

Go to the cave that's second on the left.

Find the treasure. Anyone for a plumberry sandwich?

Halloo! IDA here!

If you got to the right treasure chest at the waterfalls, it should look like this:

You are now arriving at the Diskko Desert. Land Sleepy Sheep on this flat rock.

Use the compass to find the right directions.

Go north to the fallen porridge palm tree.

Go east to the pointy rocks.

Go south to the oozy pond.

Go west to the porridge-seller's tent. In there, you will find the next treasure chest.

The porridge is delicious, especially with a sprinkling of sand.

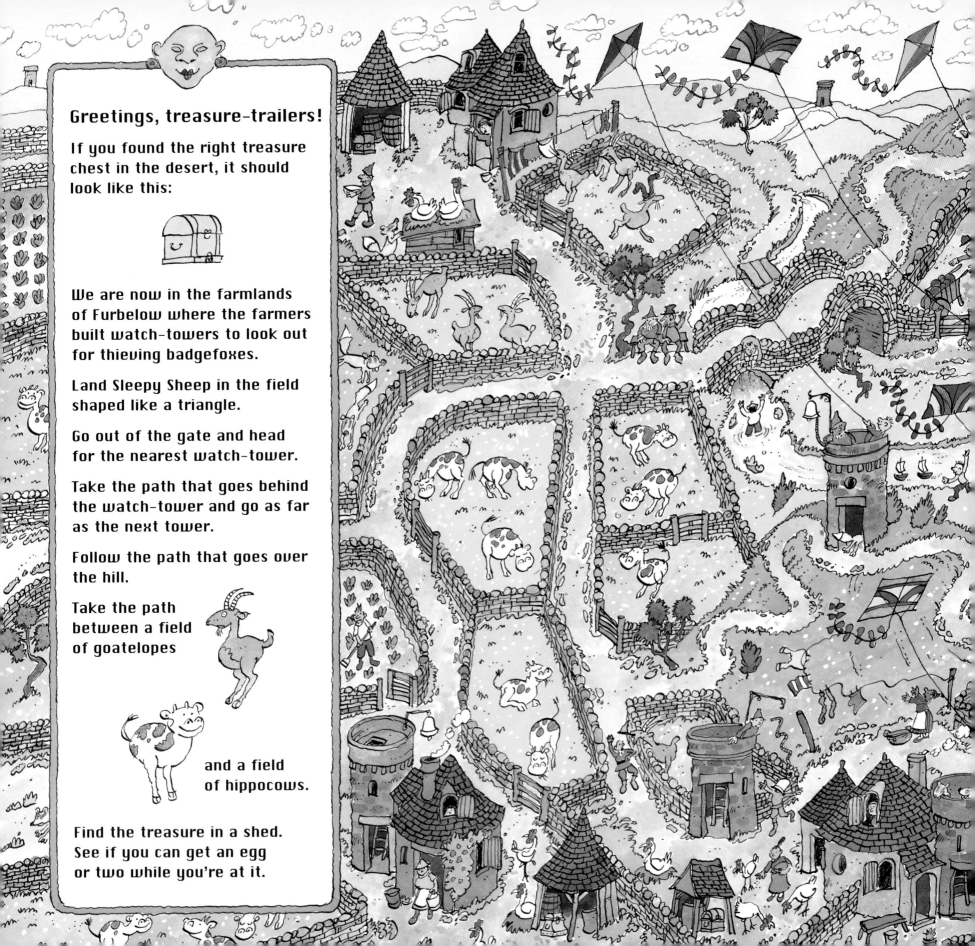

Greetings, treasure-trailers!

If you found the right treasure chest in the desert, it should look like this:

We are now in the farmlands of Furbelow where the farmers built watch-towers to look out for thieving badgefoxes.

Land Sleepy Sheep in the field shaped like a triangle.

Go out of the gate and head for the nearest watch-tower.

Take the path that goes behind the watch-tower and go as far as the next tower.

Follow the path that goes over the hill.

Take the path between a field of goatelopes

and a field of hippocows.

Find the treasure in a shed. See if you can get an egg or two while you're at it.

Howdie, pirate pals!

If you found the right treasure chest in the farmlands of Furbelow, it should look like this:

Below is a map of the Layzee Lagoons. Use it to help you find the next treasure chest.

THIS MEANS LIGHTHOUSE | THIS MEANS MUD | THIS MEANS SAND | THIS MEANS PEBBLES

Land Sleepy Sheep beside the lighthouse marked X on the map.

Walk to the end of a sandy beach.

Take a boat across to the round island.

Hop across the stepping stones then walk to the end of another sandy beach. Pick up the treasure in the lighthouse.

Bring me back two jellyfish pies, please.

BOAT HIRE

BOAT HIRE

JELLYFISH SCOOPS FOR HIRE

BEST JELLYFISH PIES Sold Here!

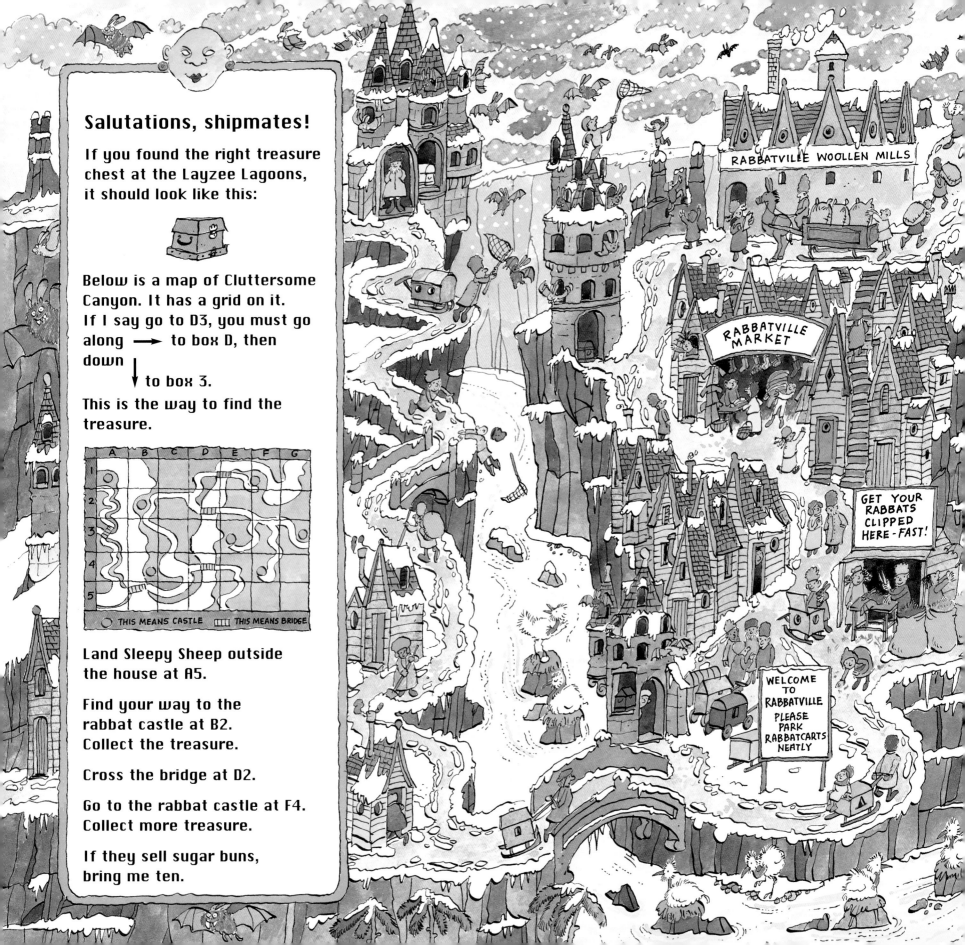

Salutations, shipmates!

If you found the right treasure chest at the Layzee Lagoons, it should look like this:

Below is a map of Cluttersome Canyon. It has a grid on it. If I say go to D3, you must go along ⟶ to box D, then down ↓ to box 3.

This is the way to find the treasure.

THIS MEANS CASTLE ▭ THIS MEANS BRIDGE

Land Sleepy Sheep outside the house at A5.

Find your way to the rabbat castle at B2. Collect the treasure.

Cross the bridge at D2.

Go to the rabbat castle at F4. Collect more treasure.

If they sell sugar buns, bring me ten.

RABBATVILLE WOOLLEN MILLS

RABBATVILLE MARKET

GET YOUR RABBATS CLIPPED HERE - FAST!

WELCOME TO RABBATVILLE PLEASE PARK RABBATCARTS NEATLY

Cheers, amigos!

If you found the right treasure chests in the canyon, they should look like these:

Here is a map of the Choowell Toffee Mines. Use the map to help you find the next treasure chest.

THIS MEANS MAIN ROAD
THIS MEANS MINOR ROAD
THIS MEANS RIVER
THIS MEANS CANAL

Land Sleepy Sheep on the spot marked X.

Take the main road from the harbour as far as the crossroads.

Take the minor road that crosses the canal twice, then crosses the river. You will find the treasure in a shed.

Hope you bring back toffee as well as treasure!

Howdie-doodie, shipmates!

If you found the right treasure chest at the mines, it should look like this:

We are now near a swaggle pitch. The Swaggle Cup final is taking place. You will need something to measure with if you want to find the next treasure chest. Here is a scale.

0 1 2 3 4 5

HOGSTEPS

Land Sleepy Sheep behind the round goalpost.

From the goalpost pole, take 10 hogsteps towards bunker number 2.

Take 6 hogsteps towards the square goalpost.

Take 15 hogsteps towards the referee in the blue box.

Take 12 hogsteps towards the red referee's box. You will find the treasure in the bunker to your right.

Do you think there will be sandwiches after the match?

	HABDASH AMAZERS		MUDDYFLATTS DAZZLERS
FLIPS	5	POINTS	2
TROUNCES	11		0
RUN THROUGHS	2		5
TOTAL	18		7

REFEREE

REFEREE

Gizmo, you guys!

If you found the right treasure chest on the Swaggle pitch, it should look like this:

It's time to take a look around Muddpye Market. Use the town plan to help you find the treasure.

MARKET SQUARE
CLOCK TOWER

XX
XXX
X

■ BUILDINGS ○ FOUNTAINS ▤ STEPS

Land Sleepy Sheep under a tree beside the fountain marked X.

Go in the direction of the arrows and pick up the first treasure chest in the shop at the top of some steps.

Continue to follow the arrows and pick up treasure at the fountain marked XX.

Follow the arrows until you reach the stables marked XXX and pick up the treasure chest.

That completes the treasure hunt. Hurry up! I'm starving.